The Girl In The Pyramid

A story from: Tales of the Ascension

Chapter 1 – Fortune's Bay

The small off-white twin prop-driven plane was an uninviting, intimidating coffin to enter. Public perception of the grim anarchical organisation had taken a complete nosedive after the events of the past twenty years. *Densissimus Imminebat* had recently lost all funding. Governments were dropping them like flies, having become disillusioned with the various factions and projects the organisation stated would see through the next generation. Robert knew everyone was getting desperate. Those that had stayed loyal to the company had fallen apart, disbanded or had been overthrown, leaving chaos in their midst. Funds were at a minimum, mixed with stress, depression and war, it was a recipe for disaster.

Robert had spent the last four days travelling to the new base of operations. The flight over had been long and arduous. Threatening to break apart from the slightest gust of wind, the plane was a small flimsy thing, not like the plush luxury jets Robert had been used to in years gone by. The delicate size of the aircraft also meant that any attempt to avoid certain members of his team were futile. Much of the journey was spent in silence, only interrupted by the constant thrumming of the twin propellors outside and the sporadic pattering of rain against the fragile, peeling white-painted metal exterior.

Robert was accustomed to travelling and visiting many beautiful countries in his ancient lifetime, however much of this journey had taken place in the flimsy, tight aircraft that restricted views across the now desecrated, burning world.

Those that joined in the silence were two men and one woman, all wore the same garb as Robert, a long white lab coat that ended just below the knees, and black trousers. The first man was small and thin, completely bald save for a small bit of grey-speckled fuzz above his top lip. He looked gaunt and emotionless. Everything the dull, grey man was creepy, his cheeks had collapsed in with the skin on his face stretching tight over his skull. Sharp cheekbones threatened to cut through the thin skin. A badge with the title, Doctor Shaw Edwards sat proudly upon the breast pocket of the lab coat. Reading his name from the badge was often the only way anyone got his name from him, a quiet man who often let the more rotund of the two men do the talking for him. On the other hand, Doctor Draius Clyne was eager to please, but often outspoken and hard to contain; this was something that infuriated Robert. Doctor Clyne enjoyed his food, never passing up a chance to indulge hi self, and it was often a wonder where his neck ended, and his face began. His face was as smooth as a baby, and he was as pasty as a sheet, seemingly never seeing the gorgeous beating blood orange sun. His skin nearly blended into the slightly oversized white lab coat which almost always had ugly brown blotches and sickly yellow sweat stains decorating it. Locks of thick chestnut brown hair fell over his forehead, just stopping above a pair of chunky, round spectacles that highlighted his light brown eyes that were constantly agaze in excitable wonder. Although, while the sparkle remained, worry and dread recently spread across the young man's face.

A more isolated participant on the trip was Doctor Errinita Martina, occupying the complete other side of the plane, keeping as far away from the men as she possible could, huddled in her small chair in the corner, legs tucked tight into her chest. While she fought the same cause as those that she shared the journey with and being a part of the same team, she could not say there was anything she really had in common with these people. She wore her thick smoky, charcoal hair in a neat, tight ponytail that fell down her back. Her face was small and pinched, while her eyes were like dark spots oddly complimenting her beautiful, smooth, dark-tanned skin, with a luscious ruby mouth that was plump, barely ever letting out a sound. The only attention she ever brought to herself the entire journey came from her incessant tapping on tables, handrails, and windows with her sharp pointed dark black nails. She was a good deal younger than the other occupants within the aircraft, and Robert had to admit, she had an exotic mysterious beauty about her that he found ridiculously tempting. It was evident, however, that she never particularly trusted men, often flinching when one approached her. Robert and Draius respected her privacy. Shaw, on the other hand, often pushed the limits, having to be reprimanded by Robert a couple of times already on the trip.

Their destination, on the other side of the world, was a mystery to them. With these emergency meeting it usually was. The plane made multiple stops along the journey to refuel, but the party was never stationary for more than half an hour at a time, and the occupants were never allowed to venture more than a few feet from the aircraft, including the clueless pilot who had to be reminded at each interval. At each pitstop, Errinita would step outside to stretch her legs and smoke five different types of cigarettes. Robert could never understand why she felt the need to tarnish and destroy her lungs like this, although he had to admit, some of the scents that wafted back into the cabin did smell sweet and tempting. There were mixtures of fruits and spices, musky oaks and even some cocoa beans. It was always the horrible tar smell that lingered with him, however, filling his airways and making him gag and reminding him of the burning world around them.

Meanwhile, both Doctor Edwards and Doctor Clyne would stand at the door of the plane muttering away to one another, speculating at what this emergency calling could mean to the backdrop of the fiery sky that burned away incessantly. At times they would just stand together in the doorway in silence, looking at the carnage that littered everywhere they went, breathing in ash and smog as it fell around them. Often, Draius would attempt to reminisce about years gone by, only to be met with a cold callous glare from Shaw, quickly shutting the notion down.

Doctor Robert Fielding, meanwhile, sat in his own little bubble, rarely ever leaving his seat, twizzling away at his bushy, matted grey beard that flowed clumsily down to his waist. Itchy rich red blemishes crowded his face, coupled with wrinkles dragging across his forehead having been collected from years of pain and stress. Doctor Fielding's eyes were grey and wise, matching his rare strands of thin wispy white hair atop his head. Just looking into his eyes, people could tell they were heavy from the wisdom they carried within them, which granted him gravitas and respect. This wisdom and intellect were only reinforced whenever he spoke, his deep, wise voice easily captured an audience's attention, people clung on to what he had to say, looking for any nugget of advice and information they could take away with them. However, on this journey, at every stop he kept quiet and to himself, drowning himself in the last issue of the world newspaper that was over half a year out of date.

A familiar buzz came over the fuzzy speaker system in the cabin of the plane. Robert and his companions had been in the air now, riding uncomfortable turbulence for the past four hours, so were all understandably disgruntled and aching from sitting down for so long. The pilot's voice was a welcome break from the silence they all now found themselves in. Even Doctor Clyne had run out of conversation topics, that was how long they had all been cooped up together.

"If you look out of the left-hand side windows now, you will be able to see your destination. Ladies and Gentlemen, I am sure you will be happy to know, we are now descending and coming into land at our final stop." The captain's voice was initially hard to hear over the white noise but, after becoming used to the static-ridden speaker system, the excitable middle-aged, experienced pilot voice was unmistakable. It belonged to someone committed and passionate about what they were doing, and Robert was grateful to have this pilot with them. He did not ask questions and blended into the background well. Robert had only seen him once on the entire journey when he first entered the plane. Dressed in all navy blue, with a classic flat navy pilots cap on and various silver medals adorning the lapel of his suit jacket, he certainly looked the part. Clearly, the pilot also liked to keep on top of himself and was well looked after in these testing times everyone found themselves in, keeping clean shaven, not a speck on his clean white skin. It was no surprise the pilot had been acquired for this mission; he was the perfect fit for *Densissimus Imminebat*.

Robert could see the satisfaction upon each face within the cabin. Even Robert felt a smile cross his face, the claustrophobia had been building within the plane so it was nice to know that soon he would be out in the open air, away from everything else going on in the world, able to spread his wings and start getting things done, rather than mulling everything over in his head. It had been a long time coming, but finally he would be heard.

Everyone leaned over to the left side of the plane to peek at where they had all been summoned to. Fields of luscious dark green trees stretched for miles, reaching to the heavens to get as much sunlight as possible. They were broken up by patches of shimmering long yellow grass that swayed elegantly in a gentle breeze, invading the spaces that the trees dared not go, only stopping at the shoreline. Encompassing the endless vegetation was a line of golden sand, acting as the wall between the green and bold blue of the sea that broke up in small waves, crashing against the island, ensuring it knew that the great oceans were not that far away. From up high, it looked as though the plane would be too big for the little island they were hovering over, but as they descended, the island became larger and soon the tables had turned, and Robert wondered where exactly the plane would land.

Over the speaker, the pilot's voice crackled in, "The island, better known as Fortune's Bay, is relatively unknown to the general public, but it has been known to be used at times of great peril, for rich businessmen and great organisations to wait out coming storms. Although, they are just stories and have no substance of truth to them. As far as I could tell, the island is relatively untouched by man, although one illicit figure has always cropped up in relation to the island, someone who defies myths and legends, but has not been seen for centuries, with many even doubting their existence. The anomaly known as Father, the supposed creator of the island." A silence hung in the cabin for a moment, as another jolt of turbulence rocked the aircraft. "Ten minutes until touch down," the pilot said finally, and a crackle ended his speech.

Sitting back down, Robert waited for the plane to land, playing the words that the pilot had said over in his head numerous times. It would be too much of a coincidence for one of the bog wigs of the company to have just randomly chosen this island for the emergency meeting he thought. No, Robert concluded. It was a message. Something was happening, something big, and all the known remaining members of *Densissimus Imminebat* were being congregated in one place... but for what?

It was not until they landed, with a ferocious thud, the plane lurching back up in the air threatening to take back off again, before eventually reconnecting with the brown, dusty runway, in the middle of a glorious green forest, that Robert spoke to his rag-tag bunch of colleagues.

"Remember what we are here for. We stick to the plan. We end this." Even though he spoke quietly, his voice commanded authority. He had captivated his audience. He received grim nods from each scientist, indicating their agreement.

Eventually, the plane came to a halt, using up every inch of runway possible. Dust enveloped the entire white metal carcass and for a moment, it appeared as if the whole world had turned an ugly brown-orange hue. As the dust and dirt began to settle, the pilot emerged from the cockpit to greet his passengers, a beaming smile emerged as the door swung open, the pilot looked as fine as ever, although his hat was at an angle, having hurriedly stuck it atop his head before jumping out of his seat, revealing part of his shiny bald head.

"Might I say, it has been an absolute pleasure, and whatever you have come here for, may you enjoy it. I believe I am to catch up with you guys later on, but I have a few things to do here first so will let you be on your way." The pilot was middle-aged, but spoke hurriedly, like a child in a toy shop. He was doing what he loved, and Robert assumed, this was likely the biggest job he had ever been assigned to. Robert could only hold respect for the experienced pilot. Apart from the slightly unorthodox, bumpy landing, the pilot had done everything perfectly. Making his way to the exit door, the pilot heaved up a huge leaver, groaning as it gave way, and the door, with some effort from the pilot, opened up to the outside world. Shaking the pilot's hand on the way, thanking him, Robert at last left the confines of the plane.

In this new environment, the air was moist and sticky, sweet and thick like treacle. It was a welcome change to the gruesome, smoky air that they were used to back at home. Apart from a single piece of hastily put together grey-brown tarmac, a sea of green surrounded them with a remodified water tower acting as the air control tower clumsily placed to one side of the runway. Large windows allowed the occupants to see anything coming into the island, although they were badly smeared and grimy, having clearly not been cleaned for some time. Huge, glistening cobwebs banded the spindly pale cream bamboo legs of the tower together. The beaming orange sun loomed large in the molten blue sky directly above, beating down and scorching anything it could get in contact with, it was the first time in a long while that Robert had been able to see the sun this clearly. He was thankful for it despite feeling his skin burning from the brief contact with its unforgiving rays. Dirt was still being whipped up around the planes propellors as they slowly came to a standstill and, as uncomfortable as it was to move in the dense heat, it was necessary to avoid being choked by the looming dust cloud.

At the edge of the runway, standing up perfectly straight and still, a woman dressed all in black greeted the four scientists. She had a smooth dark complexion and short, fuzzy black hair, that curled madly untamed towards the sky. Her eyes were covered by blacked out sunglasses, covering her eyes and most of her face, bouncing the glaring midday sunlight into the faces of Robert's team so much they had to avoid looking at her as best they could. It was a wonder how she was not boiling in her tight fitting all black suit she was wearing, matched with black leather gloves and shiny newly polished black shoes.

"You are the final arrivals; everyone is awaiting you," the woman said dryly in a delicate accent that made it hard to understand whether she was being rude or was simply emotionless. Her lips barely moved when she spoke, startling the newcomers. It appeared her subtle, robotic movements did not stop with the mouth, her face still like a wax sculpture, melting only slightly on the forehead. As she delicately swung around towards the rustling dense forest of trees behind her, the entire body moved in unison, marching purposefully away, leaving the pack no option but to follow suite behind.

"That's a good start then," Draius exclaimed sarcastically. "We are late so have already lost the upper hand!" His attempts to whisper where futile, but he made sure he spoke after the guide had taken off a few yards ahead of them, there was a chance she did not hear his sarcastic outburst.

"It does not matter when we arrive, we just stick to the plan that Doctor Fielding stated." Shaw was calm, if not a little irritated; it was a wonder how he could put up with Draius for so long. He was the polar opposite to the harmless plump little man, and scared many people at how cold and callous he could often come across.

"But we do not even know why they have summoned us all here. We are going in blind to everything. It is a long shot if our plan even works! What if they already know of what we are going to say and want to stop us before we tell everyone else?" Draius was waving his hands about manically, working himself up into a mess of emotions.

"That is why we target Anastasia; she is the one wavering." Errinita spoke up for the first time to the group, standing an awkward distance apart from the rest, yet her exotic voice carried effortlessly through the gentle breeze. She sounded annoyed by this sudden doubting from Draius. It was well documented that Doctor Martina's temper was short, bit she held herself together well in this moment, despite how tired and irritable they all felt from the long journey.

"I think even she is too far gone," insisted Draius, clearly not getting the hint from the other two. He took a well-used, wretched yellow stained handkerchief out of one of the pockets of his lab coat and took it to his sweat-drenched brow, mopping up as much liquid as possible.

As they got closer to the thick trunk of trees, and long grass that separated the runway from the rest of the island, Robert turned back to the aircraft that carried them to the island. As he did, he noticed two black shrouded figures enter the cabin door that they had only a few minutes before had left out of. Robert assumed they must be helping the pilot sought some bits out. That thought, however, was dashed in an instant. A flash of brilliant white light shot from the cockpit. A tremendous bang soon followed, causing the rest of the party, to shoot back around to face the direction they had just come from. Ripples of black crows and colourful birds flew from the

14

trees in response to the deafening blow that emanated from the plane. It took Robert a minute to process what just happened, as the two figures re-emerged from the cabin of the dirty white plane, they now looked a good foot taller than when they first went in. All that could be heard now was the whistle of the island's songbirds. The grim reality of the party's situation began to set in.

"We stick to the Plan." Robert finally spoke up, rasping each word through gritted teeth. Draius hung his head, while Shaw and Errinita stared grimly at Robert. Perhaps Draius was weeping thought Robert, he could not blame the man. We finish this once and for all," Robert said defiantly, and turned his back on the plane, marching off into the deep green forest behind the guide who had not turned to stop once. Robert knew as well as anyone, this would be the end of them.

Chapter 2 – Dying Embers

Wading through waves of tall sun-bleached yellow grass, the guide silently pushed thickets of prickly nettle bushes aside, trampling on all kinds of beautiful, wild, undiscovered colourful flowers beaming bright in the scathing heat of the afternoon sun. Draius was the most uncomfortable of the lot, constantly patting his dripping forehead with his pale-yellow stained handkerchief, mopping up sweat and dirt with his chubby little fingers. On multiple occasions Errinita cussed at the ground, her chunky black boots often becoming snagged in a tangle of wafting grass and sticky vines. Whereas Robert and Shaw kept to themselves, quietly following the footsteps of the guide, if they were annoyed or uncomfortable, they did not let it show. The walk through the relentless greenery felt like an age, the orange sun visibly moving across the sky as they went. While Robert wanted to press quickly as they, it was necessary to stop on occasions. The heat was unbearable. Large tree trunks reaching 200 feet high offered reprieve from the unforgiving heat of the sun, the party would have been fools to not savour it every now and again.

"We should have been told about this," whined Draius, as the party continued to trudge through piles of leaves and broken grass. "I would have packed suitable attire if I'd have known we would be walking through a literal forest!" Nobody gave him the satisfaction of answering. He was simply met with grunts and groans as they continued deep into the uninhabitable shrubbery.

Finally, the guide stopped at a small concrete box that poked out of the ground. If someone was not looking for the concrete box, it could very easily be missed. Next to the crumbling, grey concrete shed was a large tree stump cleanly cut off about a foot above Shaw's head, exposing the beautiful cream flesh of the once proud trunk. There was no sign of the rest of the tree and no sign where the concrete shed had come from or why it was there. Automatically, once the guide was within touching distance of the box, the guide pumped in four buttons on a small silver remote she carried in her small, gloved hands. No one was quite sure where she had produced the remote from. Shortly after, with a cumbersome groan, the side facing the unorthodox party rolled open steadily, revealing a tight dimly lit cage.

"Enter," the guide ordered, standing to one side and gesturing to the small metallic cage before them.

Despite some hesitation, the group packed in, pressing awkwardly against one another. There was barely enough room to breathe as they squashed together. Once the four scientists were safely entombed within, the emotionless guide pressed a button on the remote. Slowly, the sunlight was extinguished, and the guide vanished, never to be seen again, as a concrete wall slid across, sealing the foursome into their sarcophagus. A single dim ugly orange exposed bulb sat above them, flickering away manically as the concrete tomb jolted and started its descent. The sudden, violent shudders of the lift made Roberts stomach lurch, bringing back memories of years gone by, travelling in the air as death machines hurtled through the fire-ridden skies; this time however, the coffin they were now in was simply falling, offering no way of escape if things went awry. Creaks and groans of the out-of-date mechanisms filled Robert's ears, at least it managed to drown out the incessant whining coming from Draius.

Thankfully though, the journey to the depths of the earth did not take long. Within a moment, the gentle, deep rolling one of the walls had returned and harsh, bright white light spilled back into the tight box, the wall vanishing before the groups very eyes. It took a moment for the group to adjust to the new, artificial light that greeted them. Even though they had only been exposed to the dim orange light of the elevator for around thirty seconds, the light that illuminated the new room they had been delivered too was painfully artificial and covered nearly the whole room. A harsh white, mixed with luminous orange and scatterings of green hues emanated mysteriously from the ceiling and the sides of the needlessly large room. Despite the power of the bright lights, the absolute scale of the room made it impossible for even the brightest white light to penetrate every corner, leaving ominous dark spots in the corners and back of the room where no man dared go. A worrying buzz of energy acted as background music to the room, struggling to power the intensity of the light.

Far at the back of the room, it was impossible to avoid the giant majestic symbol that adorned the back wall. It had been adopted by *Densissimus Imminebat* when they were first founded, symbolising peace and prosperity. Although, much of the world viewed it differently now, the symbols' reputation forever tarnished by the barbaric acts of the organisation that claimed it as their own. The beautifully delicate angel wings carried an enormously heavy, imposing cross that fluttered above everyone. Looking upon the huge fearsome cross gave those who admired it tunnel vision with the corners of their sight becoming blurred, forbidding the scientists to come too close. Elegant carvings decorated the wing, feathers carved into the brittle stone, the diligence and mastery was mightily impressive. A dusting of gold giving the perfect glittering finish in the pretty light that dared touch it. Robert thought quietly to himself as he stepped into the room, looking upon the Angel's Last Dance, that lauded over everyone, he mulled everything he had done under the symbol, some things good, a lot of things bad.

Monstrous incantations and shadows danced across the simple plain stone walls, stalking the perplexed group as they made their way to a long rectangular, black granite table situated in the middle of the room. While the table was unnecessarily large, it was still nowhere near filled up the room it was in. Multiple figures huddled in small groups around the table, looking bored and sombre, matching the drab atmosphere that hung everyone. Around the table were, perfectly measured stone chairs had been sculpted out of the floor. There were fifty in total, so no one around the table needed to fight for seats by the looks of things, though Robert, counting just over twenty people in the room, including some waiters dressed in smart black tuxes at the edge of the room, trying to fade into the walls behind them. On the surface of the glossy black table were white marbled lines, dancing, and weaving, and tying each position at the table to another, forming interconnected veins all across the table. A thin man, in the same outfit as Robert, but with bushy wild grey hair and a clean-shaven face was tracing the lines intensely with his small beady eyes, e looked completely unaware of where he was as he wondered if he could figure out where each spindly marbled line went. Atop the marbling were small, thick, crystal cut glasses, half-full of a delicious looking pale blue water.

So, that is what the servants at the corners of the room are holding, thought Robert. He was unsure at first due to the people in black being so far away and his eyesight not being as perfect as it once was in his aging years, but they were unmistakably clasping jugs of the pale blue liquid lose to their chests, waiting for a refill if it was ever required, silently. Pretty, faint rainbows were sent bouncing, sending ripples of much needed colour across the drab colourless room, as the white light caught the edges of the glasses brilliantly. In this light, the water looked so tempting to Robert. He was embarrassingly out of breath from the heat and the trek and had stupidly not drunk anything since the early hours of the morning, midway through their flight; he was parched. However, each glass, at a quick glance, appeared to be filled to the exact same level, and none, as far, as he was aware, had been touched. Robert was no fool. He had watched enough movies as a child and heard plenty of stories in recent years. There was no way he was going to be the first to drink out of these handily provided glasses, and it appeared everyone else gathered around the table had the same suspicions as well.

It appeared that most people around the table all had a small group they belonged to. These groups quietly were chatting among themselves, eyeing the new party up as they got into position. Only three people were without a group, isolated from everyone else, all as close to the head of the table as they could possibly be, but also, it seemed, as far away from everyone else as they could possibly be. The three of them remained tight-lipped, not saying a word to anyone, gripping their thrones tightly, staring down the table. A slightly bigger stone chair to the rest, at the head of the table, was vacant and would remain that way. As Robert and his group reached a space in the table, the room fell silent but for a distant echo of shuffling, coughs and sighs.

"Her, at the top, the red head woman with sharp black nails... she is who we are after, Doctor Maxwell-Heart," Robert whispered to Errinita as they waited for further instructions for what seemed like an age. A cold silence lingered in the room. Robert received a nod from Errinita, acknowledging what Robert said despite never looking the way of the woman. Being the last to enter the room meant opportunities to pull her to one side now would be slim, Robert realised.

Finally, the silence was broken when the slender red-haired Doctor Maxwell-Heart clapped her delicate hands together and gently uttered to the crowd that they may now be seated. Immediately, the shuffling of feet filled the room as the groups rushed to take a seat. The groups kept to themselves, allowing a chair or two to separate them from the next party. The awkward stone chairs were positioned uncomfortably close to the table and were impossible to reposition having been carved straight out of the floor. This took a few members some time to realise, with futile attempts to drag the immoveable objects out, before eventually giving up and squashing themselves into the seat. Robert looked down in dismay at the state of what this once proud organisation has now become. Once bragging the most intelligent minds of the world as members, now making do with scraping the bottom of an incredibly pitiful barrel.

"I would like to thank everyone for joining today," began the fiery-haired, slender woman at the end of the table, the only one who remained standing. As she spoke, Doctor Maxwell-Heart's beastly blue eyes darted about the room, dazzling all those who looked dared look into them. It was easy to sink into the glowing eyes. She stood at the head of the table assuredly, confidently dominating proceedings confidently, the smooth intensity of her voice carrying effortlessly in the stale, metallic air of the room. "I realise everyone had late notice, but it was imperative that this was held as quickly as possible, and in a place that could not be tracked or recognised easily."

While her opening statement was meant to be one that calmed and reassured everyone, it failed to stick the landing. Positioned under the great Angel's Last Dance symbol, it towered above her like an ugly halo, making her appear malicious and threatening, carrying a message that brought with it a thousand knives. She looked like a messenger from hell.

A small, stunted, elderly looking man stood up stiffly from his seat to replace the menacing lady with a bout of wheezing coughs. It lasted an uncomfortable amount of time. A long-crooked arm covered his mouth, yet failed to catch any of the pale sticky phlegm that flew over the table, globs visibly falling into the glass of water that sat in front of him. Eventually the bout ended, and he surveyed the individuals carefully, rocking back and forth slowly as a silence hung in the room. The man looked cruel, and it was no wonder given the unfair hand he had been dealt. One arm was considerably shorter than the other, and his pale, shiny head was large and heavy, rocking back and forth on his long neck, lacking any sort of hair. He had an ugly, pinched face, with small black dots for eyes and a small nose that only ever sniffled. Small round glasses sat atop his pointy nose. Without the funny looking spectacles, people could be forgiven for thinking he did not have eyes at all. His lips were non-existent, although his mouth was forever twisted in a wickedly gruesome smile. To top it all off, jagged scar run across the side of his cheek just under his right eye. It brought colour to his pale, ghostly skin, glowing a fearsome red.

"I would like to agree with Doctor Maxwell-Heart," his small hands gestured towards the red-haired woman now sat down opposite him. His voice was hoarse, sounding like rough sandpaper. Each sentence held a malice to it that he was desperately trying to restrain behind crooked yellow teeth. "What we are here to discuss is of paramount importance and could not be delayed. We are in crisis and need direction." The aging man lowered himself clumsily back into his cold uncomfortable seat and hung his head, taking his glasses off and wiping them upon the lapel of his pristine white lab-coat. Doctor Langley needed no introduction to the team. Whether for the right reasons, or the wrong ones, he was well known to the group. Having started out as a simple technician, he had risen through the ranks ponderously to begin with. If it was not for his experimental thinking at the Siege of Arol, he may never have been noticed. No one was quite sure exactly what happened, but rumours spread abound fifteen years ago of that fateful night, but everyone knew Langley had something to do with it. The Kingdom of Arol had fallen, disappearing into an instant, along with the royal Arol family. Emerging from its ashes, however, into the heart of Doctor Einhardt Lazeele's trusted circle, was Doctor Ashton Langley, leaching off Lazeele ever since. He knew how to maintain his position, quickly becoming Doctor Lazeele's lacky and yes man, with rumours of secret butcheries and grizzly experiments. His appearance made these rumours all the more likely to be true. A sinister silence had befallen the room.

As if rehearsed, the void the small sinister man had vacated was replaced by another ragged grey-haired man, a good foot or two taller than the previous speakers. He was larger than the other two as well, not just skin and bones but lean and trim, with broad shoulders that filled out his unique emerald-green lab coat. His wrinkled, worn face had a long bushy, grey speckled moustache that tickled his nose and finished in curled points. Above that, his eyes were a bright vengeful green that shone like streetlamps. In his prime, Doctor Einhardt Lazeele was perfectly sculpted, with his strong cheekbones and chiselled chin standing out even now behind the saggy wrinkles that now covered his face. Short, greasy, slicked back, faded black hair with streaks of grey tarnishing it, topped the man off. He seemed so cool, so calm and collected when he stood up, managing to control the room in an instant. However, when he spoke it was evident, he was masking a twitch. The left corner of his mouth spasmed after each sentence. "Doctor Langley makes this sound like it will take forever, I assure you good people, this will not take too long." Lazeele spoke with an ugly accent that ended every sentence like a definitive statement, multiplying his assuredness tenfold. A grimace permeated his face after he spoke, and a trickling ruby red river slowly dribbled out the corner of his mouth.

"It *should* not take long," Doctor Langley corrected, raising a small, crooked finger. He was braver than most, not many people ever dared interject Doctor Einhardt Lazeele.

"Well, it *will* not take long if anyone has any sense," Lazeele said promptly, looking haggard but determined. Slowly and purposefully, Lazeele rubbed his chin, looking up to the ceiling before turning his back on the table and taking a long sombre look at the great stone symbol at the back of the room. "I remember a time when no one would question us," his exaggerated gestures emphasised his points, his long arms swung like rotor blades, constantly moving as he reminisced. "We were the most powerful company in the world. Father founded this company and took us to heights no one has been before, driving us forward, mixing it up with the big guns! Some of his ideas were incredible. Father was, without question a God!

Before the dawn of the ascension, before becoming the first to ascend, he always said he would return, to walk among us once more. But what would he be greeted with? How disappointed would he be. Within the last five to ten years, we have fallen incredibly from grace. Look at us now..." he paused, turning back to his audience, "*Look* at us! Where are we now? Snivelling around in empty, desolate basements on a secret island feeling sorry for ourselves, squabbling over which route to go next!"

Disgust contorted his face in a bitter sneer. Suspense filled the room as a silence lingered in the air, every member of the room awaiting what the wise, foreign man was going to say next. Purposefully, Lazeele walked over to the great throne at the head of the table, his hard-soled black leather shoes clipping across the stone floor, breaking the deathly silence as he stood behind the throne, gripping the top of it with both hands. "I remember looking out of a window in the tallest building in the world. Golden, untouched desert as far as the eye could see. That building was the Musah Hal. Owned by the richest, most powerful people in the world, the Munshahs. Father and I would lunch with them often, the most gorgeous delicacies you could think of, rich berries, sweet nectars, oriental spices, succulent meats. It was wonderful," Lazzele's big glorious green eyes began to form tear droplets as he spoke. Quickly he brought a sharp skinny hand to wipe the wetness away, hanging his head hiding behind the throne.

No one else in the room had ever met Father. No one knew if what Doctor Lazeele was saying was true. He had been around in the organisation for longer than everyone, that was for sure, and, despite not looking the oldest, it seemed he had been around for centuries. Some even said he was Father and had founded the company himself!

Ever the storyteller, Lazeele always managed to capture everyone's imagination, and Robert saw every scientist around the long table hanging onto his every word. They all wanted to know more about the mysterious, great, Father. Robert had to admit, the magnificent tales even enthralled him. Doctor Einhardt Lazeele, the genius, the maniac… the great thespian! The only person in the freezing room who seemed disinterested in the wise man's spiel Doctor Maxwell-Heart who was analysing a black nail on her index finger, picking at it every now and again. She puffed out her cheeks and slowly fell back into the rock that was her chair, crossing her arms as she did. Robert studied her out the corner of his eye, she knew something no one else did, he was sure of it.

"We had a vision, the Munshahs and me, for what we wanted for not only the world, but the people on it," Lazeele continued, shooting back up and moving around the table as he spoke, all trained eyes in the room latched on to him. "We worked day and night at the very beginning, forming tight bonds and connections with rest of the world. And from this hard work we discovered a mineral. This mineral would be the answer to all our problems, world hunger, global warming, and *mortality!*" As soon as that final word was uttered, a chill went down Robert's back. It was not only him that felt the cold shoot up the spine. A lot of the table started shuffling around uneasily, realising where Doctor Lazeele was now going. From what Robert knew, the discovery of this mineral was nothing new. It had been around for as long as Robert had been a part of *Densissimus Imminebat*. Doctor Einhardt Lazeele himself was the one to discover it a near fifty years ago. Robert still remembers the news breaking in the world newspaper. Green rock was splattered everywhere. Questions hung over the origins of the new mineral, had it fallen from the sky? Was it secretly synthetic? Had aliens placed it here? There was a curiosity that rocked the world, and it shot the organisation to fame. However, that was short lived. Rumours abound about what started the demise of *Densissimus Imminebat*, almost all point to the discovery of the Lazeele mineral as the starting point. Nervous mutterings began, and Lazeele noticed this with some annoyance. In response, he snapped his fingers. A loud crack travelled throughout the room. Nothing happened to begin with, then slowly, the clicking of a mechanism burst came from the middle of the table. Along with the sound came a rumbling from the shiny black table. Robert noticed in the centre of it a large hatch had emerged from nowhere. Within the hole that it left, a bright green glow was emanating. It was magical and it filled the room as it gently emerged from the middle of the table on a thin metallic pedestal. A few of the people around the room shielded their eyes as the mineral attacked them with its incredible emerald glow. But it did not last long, eventually subsiding to a tolerable level. Einhardt Lazeele was grinning maniacally as he looked upon the jagged rock now sat proudly in the middle of the room, his expression bathed in the fabulous green hue.

"Now, since the mineral was discovered to be in existence, we have had certain members of the *Densissimus Imminebat* follow their own desires. And, well, we all know what has happened to us since. We had world leaders in the palm of our hands, countries doing our bidding, the world at our feet. And now… we are scrapping around for any funds we can get when there is nothing left! This mineral is the key to it all, it can get us back on the main stage of the world once again.," Lazeele was almost shouting his words at the group now, the ugly green light cast onto his face was showing his true colours it seemed. His arms were going crazy as he spat, pointing, and hissing at the mineral and at his audience. "However, there is not enough for it to go around. We need to have one project, one goal to use this mineral on, otherwise we risk destroying everything if we try and split it up." Doctor Lazeele's face had gone a pale red as he was finally now able to breathe. A pulsing turquoise vein on his right temple was starting to bulge, wriggling away furiously. He took a gulp of air and slumped into his throne of rock, puffing out his chest for one last statement, "This has got to end, we need to rally together, be on the right side of history and save humanity!" Finally, Lazeele rested. Blood was now dripping rapidly from the corner of his mouth. Red and deep brown speckles dotted his lab coat and began to pool and infect the sleeve of the white coat as he dabbed his lips with it to stem the gory red tide.

Silence descended once more. Everyone was taken aback, mesmerised by the ugly, beautiful, odd looking green rock that was now awkwardly perched on the table. Robert had to give it to the strange, imposing, foreign man, he gave the opening statement his all. Robert could see a few of the scientists that had come out of their trance nodding to each other, beginning to believe in what Lazeele had said despite their previous misgivings. Even the usual cruel-faced Shaw was enthralled by the passion on display, allowing a harrowing smile to cross his lips as he nodded his approval.

Abruptly, the fiery red-haired lady opposite Doctor Lazeele jumped out of her chair, slowly clapping her hands together in sarcastic fury. "Well, as I am sure you have all gathered after that... rousing speech, we are here to discuss the direction, no, the future of *Densissimus Imminebat*." Maxwell-Heart spoke mockingly, her eyes on Lazeele to begin with, but slowly turning her attention to the rabbiting crowd, silencing them quickly with the inflamed expression on her beautiful face. "If we make the wrong decision today, we are no more." The disdain was thick in Doctor Maxwell-Heart's voice. She looked around at the sad company she held and was losing hope in front of everyone's very eyes. Robert though he knew not why, he knew she had fallen out of love with the company some years back. The rumour mill had been in full swing once again, with news that her daughter had gone missing, and during some sort of experiment, the young girl, no older than five years old, had gone missing. Robert had to admit, if that was the reason, he could hardly blame her, especially since, at the heart of the rumour, were Doctor Ashton Langley, Doctor Einhardt Lazeele, and the Lazeele Mineral. Ever since that fateful night, Anastasia Maxwell-Heart has become more and more isolated from the upper echelons of the organisation, pushed further to the side like an annoying forgotten toy, fighting a losing battle against the elite. Although it seemed quite a stretch to Robert, he did notice that Maxwell-Heart never set eyes upon the green rock proudly displayed on the table. Robert also noticed her plump bottom lip quivering in the ghastly green light that invaded the beauty of Maxwell-Heart's perfect pale pink round face. What she said, however, clearly moved the audience, with more babbles emerging around the table; a war was brewing.

Surprising everyone in the room, someone further down the table decided to impose themselves on the debate. A young dark-skinned man with brilliant brown braids, populated with gorgeous multicoloured marbled beads, that travelled down the length of his back, stood up from his chair and rubbed his back. His booming voice effortlessly filled the room, "I mean no disrespect to anyone around this table, I merely want to speak the facts, but if my memory serves me correctly, we are only in this mess due to what Doctor Einhardt Lazeele and Doctor Anastasia Maxwell-Heart have put us through." He paused for a moment, his large lips were dry and cracked, and he rubbed his hands together slowly while he spoke in an attempt to calm himself while he thought of how to phrase his next sentence. The young scientist spoke with confidence, yet he was rattling like snake, shivering uncontrollably. Yet, he carried on, "Now, forgive me sir and ma'am, but others and I know about your various experiments as you like to call them, and that is what has toppled governments and turned the entire world against us. So, my question is, why should we trust you with the future of our company?"

The poor man did well, thought Robert, recognising him in previous events he had done as Doctor Tyrell Leadley. Robert had never seen him so terrified, however. His fear was understandable though. Robert had a horrible feeling that Leadley's days were now numbered. Leadley's dark brown eyes, the same beautiful smooth brown as his skin, were darting around the table looking for support. His gaze was met by no one, however, not even Robert. Sweat was dripping from his forehead, and he quickly mopped it with his white sleeve, panting as he sat back down.

Looking at the far end of the table, Robert could see Lazeele slouched back in his chair smouldering with rage. He clearly did not take kindly to this new person interrupting the flow of the meeting. What Robert noticed, much to his amazement, was how small Lazeele looked, being swallowed by his stone chair, being faced with something he clearly was not prepared for.

Chewing on his cheek, Lazeele let the audience wait for a response. His hands were clasped in his lap, thumbs twiddling, the fire in his furious green gaze locked on Tyrell Leadley, far down at the end of the table. How small they all looked. *How pathetic!*

Slowly, Lazeele stood up from his back-breaking chair and leant forward on the table, "Tell me, what is your name?" He spoke softly, barely above a whisper, and many people did not hear what he said, but, importantly, Leadley had heard.

The question had taken Leadley by surprise, indeed it took everyone who heard it by surprise. This strange, wise old doctor knew near enough everything about everybody. It was what made him so dangerous. Yet, here he now was, not knowing someone.

"My name is Tyrell Leadley, Sir. Head of the Tritchromane project." The dark-skinned man stood up proudly but stammered his response.

"Tritchromane..." Lazeele stroked his faded black moustache with care as he pondered his response, his face wracked with confusion adding more wrinkles than there were before. He leaned over to Doctor Langley and whispered something in his large elephant ears. Langley looked almost shocked, but then nodded and smiled. Clearly it just took some time for Lazeele's message to register. Then, Doctor Lazeele stood up, straightened his khaki green lab coat and strode for the sliding doors that Robert and his crew had entered in.

"We will pause the meeting here, for now," Langley shouted across the table, taking everyone's attention away from Lazeele. "There is something he must do, but your questions will be answered upon his return. Please remain in the room, the break shall not be long."

"What?" Maxwell-Heart was astounded. "He can't do that!" She exclaimed.

She was not alone in her annoyance. The whole room seemed fit to burst.

"Come on, we have not got time for this," Robert complained, turning around to finally confront the escaping Lazeele. However, Lazeele was nowhere to be seen. He had simply vanished. It would have been impossible to reach the elevator door in that short amount of time, surely, thought Robert. Alas, however, he was not in the room that was quickly descending into chaos.

Chapter 3 – This World Is Not Made For Good Men

Annoyed grumblings broke out from every corner of the table as groups turned to one another eagerly discussing what they had just heard.

"They cannot be serious!" one group exclaimed.

"He is losing it! I guess it really is no surprise, he must be over a hundred years old!"

"Where the hell did he go?"

"I have had enough of this already," others muttered.

"Did he really not know who Leadley is?" Draius asked, posing the question to no one in particular.

"It would seem that way," Edward Shaw replied dryly, not looking the least bit impressed. He leaned over Draius and whispered to Robert, "I suggest we make our move now. Maxwell-Heart is alone right now."

Robert nodded his approval of the suggestion, "Yes, you are right, we just do not know when Doctor Lazeele will return so better move fast."

In unison, the team of four rose out of their seats. A few of the other groups had already stood up and were walking around the room, stretching their weary legs. They had to pass a few other groups before they reached Anastasia who was all the way on the other side of the table.

"Let's do this then," Robert said under his breath and marched along the never-ending table. He shielded his eyes as he strode past the blinding shimmering emerald mineral, Robert feared if he looked upon it for too long, it would away sweep him. Alas, it appeared that Edward Shaw had been poisoned by it already. His scheming black eyes were being tainted by swatches of green that seeped out, penetrating both his iris'.

"Robert is that you?" came a high-pitched shout from behind. Two short ladies were fast approaching the pack. Both wore oversized lab coats that trailed behind them on the dusty cold stone floor. On the lapel of their lab coats they had matching shiny, polished golden pins depicting two sharp pointed arrows. They were beautiful ladies, and Robert recognised them in an instant. It was hard not to remember a gorgeous lady with blonde hair that would often show a bit too much attention to you in lecture theatres that Robert used to work at. The just as beautiful, tanned bronze girl next to the voluptuous blonde was her friend; it seemed after all these years they were still inseparable. Both carried large innocent smiles with them and were a good twenty to thirty years younger than Robert. Their pristine skin yet to show any signs of wrinkles despite the stressful time everyone was now in; clearly, they had cashed in favours to remain in their privileged lifestyle.

Robert blushed as they came up to him and gave him a hug one at a time, a smirk crept across Shaw's face. "Ladies, how lovely to see you again after all these years," Robert tried pushing them off.

"Oh, isn't it just! To think it has been nearly thirty years since you were teaching us history! What was it you were so passionate about? Oh, I have it, the Battle of Coshtravnosh!" The woman's blonde ponytail whipped around nearly striking Draius' love-struck face. She spoke in a sickly-sweet manner, bubbly and carefree, lifting the spirits of everything around her… well almost.

"Yes, yes, look I really cannot talk at the moment. I promise I will find time to chat!" Robert said hurriedly.

"Oh, no it is ok, I can speak to Doctor Maxwell-Heart," Clyne offered, with a condescending pat on the shoulder. However, behind him, Errinita's eyes widened at the prospect.

"No, I really think Robert should handle matters, we can speak to his... acquaintances?" She struggled to find the word, maybe it was because English was not her first language, more likely, however, it was because the look on Robert's face.

"No, I will speak..."

"Come on, it is Robert's plan he should do it," Draius sprung to life, sensing the annoyance growing within his friend, Doctor Edwards. What was so important to Shaw to make him so keen to speak to Maxwell-Heart? He had shown no interest up until this point, he was only here because Clyne had convinced him, practically dragging him along.

"Well, are you not going to introduce us to your party, Sir," the smaller of the two girls, pale with short black hair that fell cutely over her small round face, giggled. Her voice was harmonious and melodic, as if she was about to sing. It had an elegant smoothness to it, much like her whole look.

Robert shuffled uncomfortably. He did not like how she called him Sir, he had not heard that in... well, nearly two decades! "Um, well, yes, of course. This is my team, the tall man on my left here is Doctor Shaw Edwards. He was

Technical Lead in this handsome chaps Bomber Development team a few years back," Draius Clyne beamed from ear to ear as Robert gestured at him. The girls in front giggled in delight, as Draius wiped his long brown fringe to one side, taking a long look at the gorgeous women. Shaw glared at the floor throughout. Unfortunately, Robert had very little he could say about the unapproachable man, and the less said about him, the better, he thought. "I first worked with Doctor Draius Clyne back when we had just developed the Hydraform, a beautiful little device that could telepathically link people within a certain radius. It took months to refine, but it was very successful."

"Apart from a hiccup in Arol," Clyne butted in, trying to make himself more noticeable to the grey and orange gaze of the two ladies.

"Yes, but I did not think we needed to mention that" scolded Robert. And, finally, we have Doctor Errinita Martina. We have only conversed over calls, but from my small research on this most remarkable woman, she took the lead in the Phalltract project," at that, Robert saw his student's eyes light up.

"No way, that is so interesting to me," the blonde girl said, looking in awe at the tall charcoal-haired lady in front of her.

"I can tell you all about it if you like," Errinita laughed to herself. It was actually pleasantly nice to speak to someone interested in her line of work, and another female presence always helped.

"That accent? Where are you from?"

"She is from the Isle of Vantrest," Robert interjected, "And, team, can I please introduce, Polly Fortrais" he gestured at the gorgeous blonde who held her dainty perfectly manicured hand up to wave at the group, "and Millie Sarth." The slick black-haired girl beamed from ear to ear, her sweet red smile was intoxicating, "They were my students at the University of Dardenelle some years back."

"Doctor Fielding's best students I would like to add," Polly jumped in, "I must say my favourite lecturer, he actually made history fun, despite his distaste for all the violent episodes." Polly said with a coquettish grin. Her face made a range of exaggerated playful expressions as she spoke, making Errinita laugh.

"A lecturer as well!" Doctor Edwards whispered dryly in Robert's ear, "what can't you do? Well, run along, don't want to miss your chance with your main lady now do you?" Disdain covered Shaw's face as he sent Robert along with a gentle, yet abrupt, shove.

"Oh, uh, yes, I promise I will catch up with you," he directed at Polly and Millie. Both girls waved at him and then directed their full attention on Errinita, pressing her about her project. It was certainly fascinating, all about various flowers and how they could be transformed into various energy sources and weapons. At least they had Errinita to converse with. Robert would have bene uncomfortable leaving them with Shaw, and Draius, well he was too busy ogling at them to make any meaningful conversation with.

With that, Robert finally made his way to Maxwell-Heart. It did not take him too long to reach the woman who had sunk into her chair, fiddling with a pen in her long, posh pale fingers. Having at first been irate at the sudden departure of Lazeele, she quickly became disinterested at the chaos that ensued between the various parties, arguing amongst themselves. Maxwell-Heart was making no attempt to join in any conversations with any of the groups dotted about the giant room, something that Ashton Langley was doing. The small, impaired man seemed to have become friendly with a group of similar looking, old haggard men, chatting away to them about his "marvellous" accomplishments. *I bet he leaves the "good" bits out*, thought Robert.

"Miss Maxwell-Heart, could I have a moment of your time?" Robert asked sheepishly, clutching a seat to the left of her, just out of Anastasia's vision.

"Would it matter if I said no?" the slender red-haired woman answered coldly from her frozen stone throne.

"Well..." Robert was not sure how to answer that.

"Oh, just sit down and get this over with," Maxwell-Heart cut in "I have nothing else to do." She exasperated. Robert worried he had already antagonised her. "What is it?"

Robert quickly sat down in the vacant chair next to the tired woman. As his rear touched the stone, a pang shot through him, not at how cold it was, but something else. It felt like electricity! He rubbed his rear with a wrinkled hand and slowly lowered himself back down. This time, nothing happened. *How strange*.

This close, Robert noticed large blackened purple bags underneath Anastasia's exotic ancient blue eyes and worried wrinkles crease her forehead. She had been through so much, she looked ready to give up. It was a worrying sight, not just for Robert's plans, but to see someone this low.

"Well," Robert began, clearing his throat of clumps of sticky, grim phlegm, "I will keep this short,"

"Thank God,"

"Yes, well... basically, I have been doing some digging. Nothing illegal, but it is my responsibility as the only remaining member of the Peace Board to look through certain files of various colleagues in the organisation..."

"You mean the various *remaining* colleagues. I suppose your job has become a lot easier recently, less people to vet and root through," her facetious responses went unremarked by Robert. He pressed on.

"Well, I thought you should know, I found something very disturbing when going through the files of Doctor Lazeele. He is not who he says he is. He is bringing this world to its knees, and he will stop at nothing to achieve it. I know it seems obvious but, I have evidence of atrocities he has committed, the Siege of Arol being one. And this rumour about the Girl in the Pyramid, he has been searching for it in the Caves of Cartuhn, and the reports are horrifying what they go through. Creatures he has created. It is everywhere in these documents I have uncovered. Everywhere he goes, everything he does, everything he is doing, he leaves a trail of death and destruction…" Robert could feel himself boiling with rage and passion as he went on. However, these feelings were not being reciprocated by Maxwell-Heart.

"And why are you telling me this?" Anastasia seemed unmoved by everything Robert had just said. She was sat, elbows resting on the glossy black table, head in hands, rubbing her temples impatiently.

"Well, I need your help to stop him, depose him, take away his power. You have control of the policing force on Tranquil Island, do you not? You could arrest him?"

"We are not on Tranquil Island, not sure if you have noticed." She never lifted her eyes from the table.

"But we have to do something." Robert insisted. He was flailing badly, desperately searching for a way to talk her round.

Anastasia did not reply for a while, she was impossible to read. Slowly her head came out of her hands, and she took a deep gulp of air, exhaling loudly as her back hit the back of the stone behind her. She turned to face Robert, "Have you read my files?" Her eyes fixed on Robert's spectacled grey face. Her voice was barely above a whisper.

"Well, briefly, yes, but..."

"You know what I have done?"

"Well, some of it," *Is she interrogating me?* Robert was confused at what was happening.

"Whatever you have read, it does not even attempt to scratch the surface. I have caused atrocities. Countless people have died in my name. You mentioned Tranquil Island, yes? It is destroyed. It is gone. What I did there was unspeakable. Some could say it was justified, it can never be justified, though. Whatever you think Lazeele has done, I have done so much worse. The only difference between me and him, he can live with it."

Robert did not know what to say. What could he say? Anastasia fell back into her chair and shut her eyes.

"Now, leave me Doctor Fielding. If you want a job, search for my daughter. Do that for me and pray Lazeele does not hold her," She paused for a moment and breathed deeply, her nose hissing like a snake as she did. "You are a good man, but good men do not belong in this world. I wish you the best."

Robert sat for a moment, looking upon the sorry state of a woman Anastasia was. She was defeated, and by the looks of things, possibly dying. What had happened to the great, inspiring woman that had once been. When she first joined *Densissimus Imminebat* she made shockwaves. She was revered by the public, a stunningly fresh-faced woman with great new ideas, propelling the world to a new golden age. This image, in front of Robert now, was not that same woman.

Sorrowfully, Robert stood up from his seat and stretched. He did not say anything to the sleeping skeletal woman. Instead, he made his way back to his party. They had just been approached by one of the faceless, black-tuxed servants. It seemed as if everyone was making haste to their seats.

Robert was the last to return to his chair. This time, thankfully, there was no electric zap to shock his backside.

"How are Millie and Polly?" He asked Errinita.

"They are lovely, and they gave you a glowing review. Made me a little jealous that I was never in your lectures," Errinita replied with a small smile creeping across her luscious lips. "Polly said she has a family awaiting her return and Millie said she is expecting!"

"Oh really, she does not look it." Robert said shocked. She had always been plump; Robert had just assumed she had never lost the weight. He looked across the table and a beautiful smile across the bronze girl's face greeted him.

The cute woman was made for motherhood, Robert always knew it. A sad smile befell his face.

"Well, how did your chat go? Do we have her on board? Will we finally remove that wretched man?" Errinita's face quickly turned to a scowl just thinking about Doctor Lazeele.

Robert could not look Doctor Martina in the face. Instead, it hung to the table.

"Well?" Draius piped up now, sensing something had gone awry.

"I fear we have underestimated our enemy," Robert muttered grimly.

Shaw tapped Robert on his shoulder, "It's ok. I know the truth as well. It has all been taken care of. I spoke to one of the servants." He tapped his nose cockily, a wry grin crossing his usually dead-pan face. It did not suit him. Robert looked at the odd man puzzled, as did Errinita and Draius.

"They are all one and the same at the end of the day, are they not?" Shaw continued cryptically, slowly revealing a small glass vile from his top pocket. It had been cracked in half, jagged points cutting into the tip of Shaws' finger, some odd blueish residue still left within dripped onto the table, running down the white marble lines trying to escape the room. It was poison!

Robert looked the fool directly in the face, his eyes wide in panic and astonishment, "What the hell have you done?" He exclaimed.

"Putting things right." Shaw replied calmly.

"You idiot! You have killed us all!"

Then, a crack appeared in the wall underneath the imposing symbol at the back of the room. More glowing green light spilled into the room, tarnishing the whole room. It now looked more like a horrible night club than it did an underground bunker. Smoke poured out of the hole in the wall, and within a dark silhouette emerged. Even before the hazy white smoke had dispersed revealing who the lanky silhouette belonged to, everyone knew Doctor Einhardt Lazeele had returned.

Chapter 4 – The Ascension Cannot Save Us All

Nervous fidgeting echoed between the cold, damp uninteresting walls. A deathly silence soon followed. In unison, as if controlled by a master controller, the featureless, robotic servants stepped forward from the edges of the great meeting room to top up the glasses that all sat rigidly untouched on the table. None of the glasses needed it, but each one got a top up, nonetheless. An unmistakable, wicked smile crept across Shaw's stony face as his cold pins watched Maxwell-Heart's glass fill to the brim. As the lifeless water-bearers stepped away into the shadows of the room once more, Doctor Einhardt Lazeele, having taken up his seat opposite the fiery-haired Maxwell-Heart, pulled out a large wad of paper from a brown paper folder he had brought into the room.

Lazeele's face sat unmoving. His green eyes darting over the contents of the paper folder, flicking through numerous pages in rapid motion. A snake tongue protruded from the long man's thin lips, licking the corner of his mouth, soothing it from a vivid red colour where he had chewed away at the flesh to a calmer pink. Satisfied with what he had read, he set aside the large wad of paper and produced a small white envelope from within the brown folder. Sharp pointy nails satisfyingly sliced open the seal and, between a bony index finger and thumb, Doctor Lazeele produced a small, shiny golden ring. Embedded within the lavish ring were a number of precious gems, the most prominent being a coruscating lilac. The glorious ring caught the brilliant glow of the mineral sat in the table, bewitching everyone around the table as Lazeele held it up proudly.

"Now, I want to apologise for my swift absence. I hope I did not keep you waiting too long but the... *gentleman* over there had reminded me of something." Lazeele began, waving his hand about apathetically in the direction of Tyrell Leadley. Robert rolled his eyes at this. "It is important for you all to understand our roots, where we come from, what we have *always* striven for. This ring here, was one of *Densissimus Imminebat* first creations. Something Father had been working on for some time and something he sought to perfect right up until his ascension," Lazeele's spoke harshly and with contempt. His alluring story-telling form before had passed, not attempting to capture the interest of anyone, instead demanding it now as he spat is words out, fiddling with the lavish ring between his fingers. "Known as the Alphillio Ring, many theorised it descended from the Armaic God. Father was happy to run with that theory. He did not want the everyday person to believe such power could be man-made. The secrets of the ring have forever been held secret, Father took them with him when he ascended, but it is said that people's truest desires are discovered when they put on the ring..."

Everyone awaited Lazeele's next sentence. But it never came. The idea lingered in the audience's minds for some time. Then, it dawned on Robert that, nothing that the elderly man had said, had anything to do with what had been posed to him before he left the room some thirty minutes ago. Perhaps it was his age, and he was becoming confused. Where was he going with this? Robert looked around the room. Slowly, he began to see this thought dawn on the other scientists that shared the room with him. And everyone was coming to the same, horrible conclusion as Robert. This diversion of the topic was not unplanned.

A delicate tinkle tickled the ears of the occupants. Shivering throughout the room, the glossy black table attacked the fragile ring as it hopped across the long slick surface until it eventually came to a spinning stop in front of a wide-eyed, plump bronze woman. She stared at the luxurious ring, sat right in front of her, nearly under her nose. It was like the ring was teasing the poor woman.

"You," Doctor Lazeele hissed, pointing a sharp finger at the bronze girl. "Go on, put it on. Let us see your desires, Doctor Sarth."

Millie began to tremble. Maybe it was from the nerves of being acknowledged by the great Doctor Einhardt Lazeele, or maybe it was from the uncertainty of her new predicament, being put on display in front of all of her peers. A trembling hand reached out, her pudgy fingers grasping at the small ring in front of her. Robert wondered how the ring would even fit on her fingers, the ring seemed a better match for slender fingers. This thought had clearly crossed Millie's mind as well as her worried pale grey eyes shot to Lazeele, a glistening fluid filling them.

"Go on, put it on any finger," Lazeele encouraged, becoming impatient with the woman. Despite speaking down the long table, he never once raised his voice, yet everyone could hear him clearly.

A reassuring stroke of the shoulder from the blonde Polly eased Millie's nerves. To Robert's surprise, the ring slipped right on with absolutely no resistance. It was incredible. Millie massaged the ring as it sat snugly on her middle finger, holding her right hand out to admire it and show the intrigued onlookers. The ring dazzled like never before, seemingly taking on its own glow, overpowering the green shine of the mineral in the middle of the table.

Lazeele sat back in his chair grinning cunningly, rubbing his bony hands together in glee, "Now, let us see what Father had uncovered."

For some time, the table sat, unmoving, waiting patiently for something to happen. An air of expectancy hovered over the group as they watched the ring and the striking lilac rocks that adorned it. Robert even noticed a couple of the people around the table yawn, becoming tired of this fiasco.

Then, suddenly, Millie gasped. A sharp intake of breath startled the room as Millie shot upright. Her face was one of amazement and shock, bewilderment and longing. She seemed to be shining, emitting a heavenly pure light. Millie's nervous shaking had stopped, instead it had been replaced by an alien, worrying twitching as she struggled to remain still. It seemed like she was convulsing in fits of pain, but rather than keeling over or trying to comfort herself, she was being restrained against the back of her chair. It was a harrowing sight.

"Millie, Millie can you hear me?" Lazeele shouted over the table.

"Yes," Millie replied immediately, her voice high and squeaky.

"What do you see, tell the room what you can see," Lazeele commanded.

Millie's eyes were darting across the room in a complete frenzy. Her twitching was becoming more aggressive, yet her head refused to move. The pale grey eyes were full of tears, and glistening streaks littered the young woman's face.

"I... I can see my future," Millie responded. Her voice a mix between a giggle and a sob. "Fields of grass, a beautiful house, and... oh my is that? Yes, it is..."

"What is it? Tell us Millie, what can you see?"

"Oh, it's beautiful! It's so so..."

"Yes?"

"Who is that?" Suddenly, the white glow surrounding Millie turned an ugly, violent red. Millie's body below the neck began shaking uncontrollably and her arms crossed over her chest, itching at her upper arms maniacally. "No,

No. GET OUT!" She yelled, screaming at no one. Her eyes were fixed now though, staring directly at Robert. They did not move from him, locked on Robert for dear life as her body slammed against each side of the chair. Her face was contorted in a horrible sneer, screaming for help, her mouth spat out white foam as she cried out.

A few men, either side of Millie, stood up and ran over to her trying to grab a hold of the out-of-control woman.

"SIT DOWN! DO NOT TOUCH HER" Lazeele shouted.

The men looked at each other, unsure what to do but one look at Lazeele was enough to stop them from disobeying.

Polly was screaming in fear, covering her face with her hands as her friend next to her threw herself against the chair. Everyone else looked on in horror as Millie screamed at Robert.

A burning smell entered Robert's nostrils. It was revolting. The flailing woman opposite Robert was now engulfed in bright orange flames, the heat was suffocating even the people sat across the table from Millie. Everything happened in an instant, so quickly and so furiously. Her shrill screams turned to gurgles as she choked on ash and foam, the thrashing slowly turned to limp convulsions until, with a heavy thud, a black charred head crashed down onto the table. The death stare had finally ended.

Chapter 5 – Judgement

Polly wailed; her scream was blood-curdling as she looked upon what had become of her best friend. Robert was not sure what was worse, the image or the smell that had filled the previously stale room. Thankfully, what was Millie slowly disintegrated before everyone's very eyes. The charred, blackened corpse slowly disintegrating into dust. Soon, all that was left was the golden ring, sat elegantly on the table where Millie had been. It was almost beautiful as the gritty black and furious orange dust of the cadaver carried up in the unexplainable frosty breeze that travelled through the room. The stunned silence that followed was deafening. Everyone had eyes on the now vacated seat, frozen in fear. Even Polly had stopped her choking.

"What was that?" Maxwell-Heart whispered vehemently. It was the most invested she had looked for some time.

"I told you, the Alphillio Ring," Lazeele said coldly.

"No, what the hell just happened?" Maxwell-Heart screamed, slamming her fist down on the table.

In response, Lazeele simply clicked his tongue, leaning back in his chair calmly. "It was an experimental ring, meant to show you the person's truest desires. Some say it holds visions of what those who ascended have experienced. Those who have ascended hold judgement over that person. If that person's desires are true and pure, they carry on with a prosperous life. If they are deemed unworthy and impure, then... well..." Lazeele shrugged. "That is what Father was working towards. Yet, it was slightly raw in its processes, but he was getting there. That is the trouble with this company now. We simply do not see through anything and become entangled in far too many projects at once.

"I suppose, what I want to make abundantly clear is whatever Doctor Maxwell-Heart has been doing to various subjects to achieve her goals has nothing to do with me. I am working on, what I believe is the most important thing on the planet right now. I want to alter the human form, bring us out of these weak, feeble bodies and into the universe as free beings, we would become unstoppable. Immune to physical touch, physical harm, being unwell. And the Lazeele Mineral can help us achieve that. I have seen it!" Lazeele's wicked smile never once left his cracked broken lips, his hands spread out on the table scratching at it with razor sharp nails all while he spoke, leaving cat scratches all over it.

Nobody spoke. Nobody dared say anything. What they had just seen shattered everyone's precious sense of untouchability. An atmosphere of fear filled the room so thick it could be cut with a knife. Everyone had heard stories about what the world was turning to, and what certain people were capable of, but this... this was something new. No one thought Lazeele would turn on his own people. But now, it was clear; Doctor Einhardt Lazeele had gone crazy.

"You are crazy," Errinita hissed, taking the room by surprise. Every head in the room turned to face the woman challenging the mad man. The words sounded peculiar coming from her voice but landed the perfect blow. Lazeele's smile faded into a menacing glare that spanned the entire length of the table, falling on Errinita who refused to back down. From somewhere she had found courage when no one else could. Tension was rife as everyone waited for a reply.

"She is right," was the reply, but it did not come from Doctor Lazeele. Instead, Doctor Maxwell-Heart leapt in to support Errinita.

"Ha, of course you jump to *her* defence!" It was now Doctor Langley's turn to speak up. "A couple of do-gooders the both of you, too scared to push through with the ugly stuff that will lead this company into the new generation, set us free. We are here to take risks and save the world from itself. You two are everything that is wrong with this company." The small man suddenly grew ten feet it seemed. Doctor Langley's eyes were ablaze in crimson rage as he spoke chaotically, pointing at the two women with a shuddering finger. His lips quivered and spat out every word. It was an ugly sight, his babbling rhetoric sounding like cultist prayers.

"You just murdered that poor woman!" Errinita yelled, "and for what, a demonstration of the horrors we were working on before laws were introduced? These so-called projects are what took us backwards. They are what has warped this company, not us." Errinita slammed her fist on the table forcefully, making her glass of water bounce, spilling droplets of the clear blue liquid on the table in front of her. Robert shifted uncomfortably. While he wanted to commend Errinita for what she was doing, he was also very weary about the scowling gaze of Doctor Lazzeele, now taking a keen dislike to his party.

"You think that is bad? Go on, tell us Ash, tell the room what you have contributed to the cause, the greater good of the company you call it." Maxwell-Heart did not raise her voice, she did not need to. Anastasia's mocking tone cut deep into Doctor Langley's pride as Robert noticed his brow twitch each time the cruel woman mocked his name and his work, goading the stunted man. She stared directly at Langley, never dropping her cold blue eyes that now seemed to light up with an incredible spark, bringing back the furious molten waves, "Don't worry Ash..."

"You will address me as Doctor Langley, you damned abomination!" Langley interrupted incensed. He slammed his fists down hard on the table sending glasses spilling all around him. Everyone flinched nearby, scared of the wrath of the man beside them. Lazeele and Maxwell-Heart, however remained unmoved. A cruel grin just crept over Anastasia's face, while Lazeele continued to scowl between the two women that had dared to defy his authority.

"I will address you how I like, you vile creature!" Now Maxwell-Heart raised her voice, stunning the entire room as it reverberated around the walls. "You experimented on children, babies. And for what reason? Because they were easier to persuade you said, their souls were pure and would be easier to ascend the physical body." Tears were welling up in Maxwell-Heart's eyes. "You never told anyone, but we all knew you loved their screams. God knows what else you got up to in that asylum." Anastasia was furiously scratching away at the table with her sharp black nails, causing harsh indents to be carved into the table. Robert was certain he could see ugly trickles of maroon seeping from underneath the dark nail, pooling into the same-coloured grooves now in the table.

Doctor Langley's hand came crashing down on the table with such force it was certain he broke something. A horrible crunch could be heard as he brought his fist away from the black table, "Enough!" he roared.

"Yes, you are right, I have had enough," Lazeele said quietly, interrupting the squabbling pair. His face was now shrouded in an ominous darkness, shadows covered his eyes, making them stand out amongst the black emptiness. Even the green glow of the mineral had subsided, cowering away from the menacing man, "I do thank you Anastasia for such a compelling argument against Doctor Langley. But what about answering the young man's question down the table, that one down there," Lazeele waved his hand in the direction of the poor man, his face now contorted in a mixture of rage and fear.

Doctor Leadley tried to speak but was swiftly shot down by a horrific glare from Lazeele. His impatience was becoming more apparent, he no longer had time for anyone else in the room other than for Maxwell-Heart. This was his stage, everyone else was simply there to witness the execution of it.

"My apologies for not making her answer it for you sooner, I know how long you have been waiting for it, Lazeele's face wore an ugly, twisted smile never left his face, as he feigned pleasantries, attempting to mask his contempt. Surely, he must know how ridiculous he sounded, Robert wondered, especially after how Lazeele had managed to avoid answering the question himself. He turned to Maxwell-Heart, "Well, Anastasia, answer him, why should we trust you?"

"I more meant…" Leadley attempted to butt in once more.

"Yes, yes, yes, I know. Now sit down and let her answer." Lazeele commanded not even doing the man the courtesy of looking at him, instead he waved his hand again, ushering the man to down, never averting his gaze from Maxwell-Heart. Everyone else in the room was frozen, the venom from Lazeele had paralysed everyone. Rage was building in every corner of the room, but so was fear. Robert was confused, this was not how he expected this to go, Doctor Lazeele wanted this rage boiling up from Maxwell-Heart and a lot of the room, but why?

Maxwell-Heart's demeanour had suddenly become a lot more agitated. Her eyes were dancing, spitting fire, resting upon the callous grin of Doctor Lazeele, "I only want the power to stop you," she hissed through gritted teeth, leaning halfway across the table now, "You took my daughter to find a pointless mineral. You made me do unspeakable things which led us nowhere. It has taken me far too long to realise, but everything I have done in the last year has been to put a stop to you."

"Not nowhere, my dear, in fact the work you did on the people of Tranquil Island, and getting that young woman to report on it was crucial to me discovering where we could find the mineral and what effects it has upon a person when exposed to it for too long." Lazeele reached into the wad of paper that he had produced from the brown folder in front of him and revealed four small pieces of crumpled, partly singed dirty orange paper. "Within these pages I finally now know where to find the mineral. Great work on her by the way, Helen Ottowood I believe her name was, with help from the traitor who managed to escape my grasp in Arol. Funny how everything managed to converge so perfectly. It was a shame how it ended for them on that island, but it was necessary," with that, Lazeele threw the pages across to Maxwell-Heart. Bits of the charred brittle sheets crumbled off, being flung in all directions, some picked up in the light breeze and flew about the room.

"I tortured her!" Maxwell-Heart yelled in anguish.

"And, as I said, I congratulate you."

It was like watching a robot fight against human emotions, not understanding why this person in front of them was reacting in such a manner. Lazeele was surely masking their true emotions behind a façade, Robert could tell Lazeele was relishing pushing Maxwell-Heart to the edge of explosion. The rest of the room could not take their eyes off the pair waiting for the volcano to erupt, confused, curious and silent. Maxwell-Heart was grating her perfect fingernails against the table, carving ever deeper grroves down the hard, coarse object. Doctor Lazeele was sat back calmly, allowing his participant to divulge more information unto the room.

"You used me. You used my daughter."

"And you were easy to play." Finally, the mask slipped from Lazeele. His cruel smile invaded his face once more. Viscous cockiness exuded out of the tall, white-haired man. Viscous cockiness exuded out of the tall, white-haired man, "You see Anastasia, you did everything we needed you to, me and my colleagues were most impressed. You highlighted the power we can have from harnessing the energy of the Lazeele mineral, and the affect it can have on those not yet ready to embrace its influence. We need to find a way to bend the power to our will, our goals, and to do that we need to stop confusing it. Yes, it was a shame about what happened with the ugly business with the girl, but she led us right to where we needed to go. Her mind was always too adventurous for its own good. She needed to be dealt with. In the end, she dealt with herself, I never did anything to her. So, your daughter, well... collateral damage should we call it?"

Maxwell-Heart leapt up at that line, if the chair had been moveable, it would have flung back crashing to the edge of the room, instead Robert was sure he heard the stone crack a little. The entire congregation was in shock, the usually emotionless woman had been whipped up into a frenzy by the man opposite her. The cold, calculating woman had been broken down and completely destroyed brutally for the whole room to see. Lazeele was pushing all her buttons, and this played into Robert's hands wonderfully, maybe the woman would finally help Robert and his team. Then, as soon as some hope glimmered in the dark abyss, his heart sank, Maxwell-Heart reached for the glass in front of her and took a sip to calm herself down. How much she drunk was a mystery, her hand was shaking so much as she brought the glass to her lips, spilling more than she drank.

"Look, I hate to interrupt... uh, this..." Shaw's amusement at the situation was evident, but his curiosity had got the better of the man, breaking the silence of the trapped audience, "But, you speak of this mineral as though it is alive sir."

Lazeele's head snapped round to face the far end of the table, pointing a bony finger towards Shaw. Many of the other observers around the table flinched at the gesture, recoiling back into their stone solace. The enigmatic man's cynical smile plagued his wrinkled grey face with the tips of his moustache almost touching the edge of his green eyes which glowed in excitement, "Someone cottoned on, good man!" He was chuckling now like a child in a playground, "Is that Doctor Shaw Edwards?"

"Yes, Sir," Shaw did not hesitate to respond, sitting up proudly in his seat.

What a slime, though Robert. *Now what is your game?*

"Ah, yes, the quiet man" Lazeele genuinely appeared fascinated by the long quiet man. From afar he looked rather similar to Doctor Langley, just a skinnier elongated version of the man. "I like people like you, always value them on my team. Keep to themselves but often have the best minds." Caressing his chin, Lazeele analysed the end of the table, properly taking everyone in. This concerned Robert, Lazeele was a calculating man and never did anything without reason. He seemed to have a good knowledge of Shaw, who else was he aware of in his team? Shaw did not care however, sitting proudly with a gleaming smile. Next to him, Clyne was also oblivious to the danger they now found themselves in. The floppy, brown haired man rigidly sat back in his chair, eyes wide at the vacant seat next to the still distraught Polly that once housed the one-time love of his life.

"To answer your question Doctor Edwards, yes, I refer to it as a living being because, essentially, it is. I have not had the time to study it completely yet but think of it like an alien being. It does not belong here. Yet it is here! First discovered off the coast of the Dardenelles Costanal by the Arol's they were said to have unrivalled influence and powers that no one had seen before or since. The Arolian Royal Family were obsessed with it. Then, we finally got our hands on the Lazeele Mineral thanks to Anastasia and her pet project on Tranquil Island. Father and I knew of this mineral when we founded this organisation and knew of the potential it had which is why we are still working on this project today. It is said that it contains the ability to reform life as we know it, and with the way this planet is going, why not bring about this reform? However, like you and I, when we try and do too much at once we get confused. No matter how great the mind is we can never do too much at once, we get muddled. This is now what is happening with the Mineral. We cannot tame this beast while sending it down too many different paths. This is why we have stagnated as an organisation, and we are no longer of use to these governments that use to hang on our every word, well the ones that are left anyway. There is a void that is now open, and we need to take the leap and become the new power. The nuclear bomb for example, we handed the idea over to the Munshahs and they ran with it like a moth to a flame. We built Heisen III, a way to harness the energy of the sun and we gave it to the Iban which gave them the monopoly on the world for a

decade. Then enter Udon who wanted a piece of the pie. Everyone came to us!
"We prided ourselves on giving out ideas, allowing everyone else to think they had the power. We always delivered. Sitting in the back, operating in the shadows, we were the real power. However, we were working as one team then. The Lazeele Mineral was and should still be our next goal, it is the only way we could trump what we gave to Udon. We promised immortality, we have not delivered. Instead, the world has torn itself apart. Now, it is time for us to step forward, out of the darkness. We should be the ones who rule!"

Doctor Lazeele took in a gulp of air; his colourless face had taken on a shade of maroon. During the speech he barely paused blurting out his passion in maniacal, fanatical fashion. A mix of awe and petrified faces were staring at the man, now stroking his moustache. Was no one else able to see Lazeele for what he truly was? Robert was astounded at what he just heard. What was worse was some people were absolutely believing the tirade, Shaw being one of them, nodding away frantically. What Lazeele had suggested was going against everything Robert believed in, everything that the company he joined some thirty years ago once stood for.

Robert had heard enough, "I am sorry, but this cannot be. You are suggesting that we bring the world to its knees simply because we are not able to provide the next super weapon? With the greatest of respect Doctor Lazeele, but you cannot play God. If this Mineral is as powerful as you say it is, and has cognitive abilities, then we cannot mess around with it. We need to do actual testing on it before we even think of bending it to our will."

Lazeele chewed on Roberts words for a minute, allowing himself to process the unexpected robust response. He looked somewhat annoyed; this had already gone on longer than he had anticipated. Part of him, however, enjoyed everyone turning to him for answers. What made it all the sweeter was that Anastasia had faded away from the conversation. She was now slumped in her chair, being engulfed by the walls of the sculpted seat, as tears fell down her stony cheeks.

Eventually, Lazeele responded calmly, "The world is already on its knees, Doctor Fielding. I am talking about saving it. And the issue is not with testing. We know what it does, we have tested it. Tranquil Island was the test."

"And may I ask how that turned out?" Doctor Tyrell Leadley inquired from his seat, supporting Robert.

"It was necessary to erase it." Lazeele responded, irritated by the two gentlemen. He could barely see them they were so far away.

"So not because anything went wrong with the test?" Robert asked more civilly before Tyrell could interject again.

"No, nothing had gone wrong, we just did not have proper clearance from Udon," Lazeele mumbled the last part, hoping the majority of the room could not hear him.

"So, we are not pulling the strings then?"

"We are in control doctor…"

"If we were then we would not run away scared when Udon is about to figure out what we are doing that clearly was not sanctioned by them! And what was so secretive about Tranquil Island that meant we had to blow the whole place up?" Robert was infuriated at even having to ask such questions and expose such blatant truths. He did not care how much notice Lazeele took of his team anymore, it appeared he now had nothing to lose. He took a deep breath to calm himself down.

"I see," Lazeele pondered for a moment, stroking his chin, "I see why you are so concerned. What head of a peace committee in this organisation wouldn't be. I would demand answers if they were not, so good on you for that. However, I can assure you the eradication of Tranquil Island was necessary, and Udon eventually saw that this was the only way to maintain the peace on this planet. We do not want someone else being in possession of the Lazeele Mineral, only Father knows what would happen if it was to fall into the wrong hands!"

"I will not have this!" Robert erupted, "You have butchered thousands of people, and not just on Tranquil Island. Even today, in front of all of us, you murdered one of us! You have done this countless times over the past decade, killing millions, and claimed it was to maintain the peace but just sent the world and our organisation into deeper turmoil. That is why everyone has turned their backs on us, not just because of false promises. Doctor Maxwell-Heart please stand up against this. Everyone, please, he is the wrong pair of hands for the Mineral to be in," Robert pleaded desperately for someone else to come to his aid among the twenty or so people in the room he sat silently. No one dared to look in his direction, instead looking down into their glasses of water solemnly accepting defeat. His own team were pushing themselves deeper into their stone seats, willing them to swallow them up.

"Oh, I can assure you Robert, I am the right person to have it," Lazeele's face now held an evil grin. His voice deep and low, he did not care what his audience saw him as now. The pretence had ended.

"My daughter was not collateral damage," Maxwell-Heart uttered, almost hissing out the words, interrupting the confrontation between Robert and Lazeele, "You tricked her."

"I'm sorry Doctor Maxwell-Heart, I was just trying to get across why I think you should..." Robert was cut off before he could say anymore.

"Oh, please Miss Heart, not now let the grownups talk" Doctor Lazeele's relaxed tone never faltered, ignorantly flapping a hand in her direction to try and shut the woman up. However, he seemed to be the only one oblivious to what was happening opposite him. Slowly, each pair of eyes in the cold room descended upon the corner of the table where Maxwell-Heart was hunched over.

"You do not know what you have done," Anastasia croaked, "this obsession with the Mineral, the obsession with improved life, the freeing of our bodies, and yet you have missed what is needed to bring this altogether." Maxwell-Heart's greying eyes never lifted from the table, all the life had been drained from them, with dried streaks burned onto her pale white cheeks. Her feisty red hair fell over her face, usually so neat, now tangled and matted. As she slowly raised her face to Lazeele, all that remained was a cold dead stare.

"And what might that be hmm, what have all our top minds missed?" Lazeele almost chuckled condescendingly at her, looking down trying to get Maxwell-Heart to look him in the eyes. However, behind that chuckle Robert detected a slight nervousness. His control of the conversation was waning, and Maxwell-Heart was no longer following his script.

Meekly, Robert exited the conversation, lowering himself back down into his chair realising he was no longer of any concern. He was disappointed in himself; Anastasia was not listening to a word he was saying but was annoyed he could not put up more of a fight to get his views heard and considered. His plan had failed. He scratched his scraggly beard and patted away some nervous sweat from his brow that had fallen into his bushy eyebrows. Bringing his hand to the collar of his lab coat, Robert tried to loosen the grip around his neck to give himself more space to suck in the sticky metallic air. Looking at his small, bedraggled party, Robert noticed the group all shuffling awkwardly. Their faces showed hints of disappointment and misery. All had resigned themselves to failure. Only Shaw seemed content, listening eagerly to what Doctor Lazeele had to say, waiting expectantly for the next grand plan.

Robert's mouth was so dry; he was eyeing up the glasses of translucent blue infused liquid greedily. Reaching for the glass, finally caving in to his desire, was when Robert noticed the peculiar water shimmering ever so slightly, rippling cutely at the surface. He rubbed the arm of his chair to calm himself, but in doing so he recoiled suddenly, a sharp and sudden zap coursed through his finger. Every hair on his arms stood to attention and he felt a shiver rise throughout him. Suddenly, a burning sensation shot through his whole body, stiffening in his chair uncontrollably. It felt like his blood was boiling inside of him. Robert yelped in fear and pain, drawing attention to himself from those around, a few people closest to him looked over concerned and confused. Doctor Leadley was mouthing something to him if he was ok and looked down at the floor gesturing something he could not make out.

Draius leaned over Shaw whispering to Robert, "Everything ok mate, seemed like you just got a shock.

Nice try though, I saw what you were trying to do. Hard to get anything in with these guys. Was that part of the plan?"

"A shame you never actually got to your point," whispered Shaw unimpressed, looking at Robert from the corner of his small black eyes, never moving any part of his body.

"Did you shock yourself?" Errinita asked from the other side of Robert. At least she was concerned, thought Robert. Her beautiful large eyes genuinely held a look of sadness and compassion within them, unlike Shaw's. "Something feels off about all of this," Now it was Errinita's turn to yelp in discomfort. Her whole body convulsed momentarily. Robert put a heavy arm on her to try and stop her from smashing her head against the hard stone chair.

"Yes, I think I did. But it felt like electricity." Robert was puzzled, dazzled almost by the shot he had just experienced. Looking down at the floor as Tyrell had suggested he noticed it shining in a peculiar way. No, not shining, it was sparkling a beautiful blue colour, bolts spiralling and zigzagging all over.

Suddenly, another woman convulsed furiously in her chair, sending two men either side the plump woman recoiling in shock. The woman's glasses were flung across the room to the wall behind her as her head was thrown backwards to face the ceiling.

"Jenny are you ok, what is happening?" gasped the man next to the woman, her chestnut hair now stood up in all directions like little tendrils. It took the woman a moment to come back to the room, breathless and dazed.

"Did you not once wonder where she went?" Anastasia now dull eyes grew cruel, their hypnotic glitter evaporated. Maxwell-Heart and Lazeele continued their plight amidst the chaos that was beginning to unfold at the other end of the table.

"She died Anastasia, you said so," Lazeele responded, perplexed by the question.

"So, you did not stay long enough to realise there was no body?" A wicked grin crept across Maxwell-Heart's face. "Only one thing can control the Mineral. You've dedicated so much time trying to figure out what can control it, how to mould it, you have let the simple answer elude you, and then you gave it straight to me." The smug grin grew bigger and bigger until almost splitting her face in two, her cold fierce face had contorted into a horrific image. Lazeele's green eyes grew wide in astonishment. What was confronting him now was no longer Doctor Anastasia Maxwell-Heart. Something was speaking through her, something else entirely.

A low rumble began to emanate from the ground. Robert looked around nervously, looking for other people around the table that were not completely transfixed by the show unfolding at the head of the table. Locking eyes with

Tyrell, both men looked at each other, panic resonating in their faces. Roberts ears were beginning to ring, he often wore hearing aids making his ears more sensitive to disturbances and something was now messing with them. A fizzing and crackling hissed at him, getting higher and higher pitched as the grumbling from the ground got ever more aggressive. Worry and anguish scrawled Robert's face as Anastasia attempted to comfort him, to limited success.

Meanwhile, at the other end of the table, Doctor Lazeele's confidence had been drained, the control sapped from his body. It was weird, he now looked so small. He was panicking, not understanding what Maxwell-Heart was saying. He never liked not knowing something and the low hum grew along with his nervous, panic-stricken face, "Miss Heart what is going on?" Lazeele's voice cracked with fear. His head was now darting around, he was noticing the glasses hopping on the table, spilling over, the liquid pouring onto the table fizzing, sending blue sparks dancing into the air.

"You are always so careful with everything you do, but you let your guard down on the most important moment of your life. I promise you this will be your only mistake," Anastasia's demeanour had completely changed. The small sobbing woman had been replaced in an instant by a maniacal monster. Her voice was vicious, unhinged and completely inhuman. She had revealed her ace card and was revelling in having the upper hand over the egotistical man who could not hide his fear now. Lazeele slowly began backing away from the table, recoiling like the coward he truly was.

Robert turned to Errinita quietly, tapping her on the arm, "We should go before this gets truly out of hand." He turned to Draius who had heard and nodded and the same with Tyrell, but Shaw was captivated in a trance, unable to look away or hear anything. Draius tugged on the sleeve of his colleagues' coat, but he would not budge. At the second attempt, Shaw snapped at the stout little man.

"Leave me alone you fat little pig. The Mineral is here for judgement upon us all," Shaw hissed, throwing Draius back violently. The floppy haired man hit the back of his chair in shock at what just happened.

"We have to go now," Robert insisted, picking Draius up from his chair, the scraggly man still in shock, "leave him, he is gone, and I fear he has been brainwashed for some time." Draius hesitated for a moment, reluctant to leave his friend of so many years, not wanting to believe what had just happened. However, his fear outweighed his loyalty, and he began to stand up and back away from the table, heading for the direction of the elevator that they had entered the room in what felt like so long ago.

Suddenly a terrific wind burst through the room. It was bitterly cold and awfully strong, buffeting everybody. Strands of hair flew everywhere, flying up into the witnesses' faces, partially blinding some of them. Some tried to brush it out of their eyes, only for the wind to whip it straight back into them again. Shaw had no such problem, as neither did Doctor Langley, although his glasses nearly flew off his pointed nose. Robert adjusted his hair, becoming even more tangled and raggedy, pushing it out of his face to witness the most brilliant thing he had ever seen. Langley's vibrant scar had dulled in comparison to the ferocious blue blaze exuding from every pore in Doctor Maxwell-Hearts body. She no longer appeared human, spitting her words out at Lazeele, his eyes wide in disbelief.

"What is this?" Doctor Langley screamed, struggling to get his voice heard above the blustering wind coming from nowhere and everywhere all at once battering people across the room, "What have you done?" raising his hands to his face to shield his eyes from the blinding light shining from and around Maxwell-Heart.

A dazzling deep blue bolt suddenly shot from the floor, crackling and spitting up to the ceiling. Large cracks started to form in the impenetrable stone walls and concrete dust started to fall to the floor amidst all the panic. Ashen dusted people all around Robert started to choke and splutter as the wind started to suck out of the room into the cracks. The whole room was a mess of hair and flitting lab coats as people fell to the floor scrambling to the edges of the room. One man had scrambled to the wall at the back, underneath the great Angel's Last Dance, not noticing a small crack crawl its way up to one of the expertly carved, glorious wings. The only people that now remained at the table were Shaw, who was glued to his seat, Doctor Lazeele and Doctor Langley who were all transfixed by the slowly rising Maxwell-Heart.

Another zap came from the floor suddenly. Immediately everyone fell to the floor convulsing in agony. All except for Anastasia and Robert who looked around perplexed at his fellow colleagues writhing in agony around him on the floor. Anastasia's burning gaze was fixed upon Doctor Lazeele, who had also fallen to the floor on his back, contorting in unimaginable ways. A devilish grin tainted Anastasia's smooth face, leaving wrinkles sprawling across her cheeks and forehead, and the blue hue emanating from her turning her blue eyes a menacing purple colour, everything else had been drained of colour. Her hair remained still, however, at the epicentre of the storm, while everyone else's flew about uncontrollably.

"You sent her into the Magenta Sky as part of Operation Darktrace, you did not realise it was fully working though. Junie fused with the pyramid, and now all we need is the Lazeele Mineral, and you will give it to us. We will end this." Anastasia spat her words out, a mix between crying and laughter. One moment her voice was inaudibly high, the next a ground-shattering low. In the midst of the disarray, Anastasia raised her arm elegantly towards the glowing green rock. On command, the Mineral obeyed and began floating gently towards the spirit-like woman.

The room shook violently as the blue bolts blasted out from the rapidly disintegrating floor even more. Robert clung to one of the chairs, urging the rest of his party to do the same. Soon everyone else in the room started to do the same, crawling to the nearest chair through fits of convulsions, trying desperately to stay low to stop themselves being buffeted like a ragdoll against the walls. Draius had foam spilling from his mouth, his eyes bulging out of their sockets and bloodshot, one had turned completely red, while Errinita's hair had frayed and fizzed, standing up on end with a thick oily substance spilling from her both ear. Tyrell's lab coat seemed to have singed at the collar and cuffs, and he was limping as he struggled to get to the table in the centre of the room. Viscous crimson liquid trickled from noses, ears and eyes, as vibrant as Doctor Langley's scar. He was the only one other than Robert, Doctor Lazeele and Doctor Maxwell-Heart who seemed to be immune to the bouts of agonising convulsions. However, Langley was in utter disbelief, staring directly at the people on the floor, utterly motionless, his hands pressed tightly against his ears and his eyes slammed shut, attempting to block out the unbearable screaming as ferocious flames were introduced to the bedlam.

Robert could hear an enormous thumping coming from nowhere, but everywhere. He was unsure whether the depths of hell had opened beneath them or if it was just the beating sound of his heart. He was breathing heavily, struggling to catch his breath as the gale tore throughout the room ever faster with every passing second, stealing away the preciously sweet air. He was sure his heart was pumping heavily, rhythmically in time with the low hum and rumble of the viciously punishing floor. With that came an ear-piercing, screeching whine that blew some people ear drums in a gruesome mess that decorated part of the walls. The neatly laid out glasses had all smashed, sending shards of glass hurtling at people, one of the servants' throats was severed resulting in a crimson sprinkler dousing those nearby as he gurgled and fell to his knees, a hand scraped at the gash, failing to stem the flow. Another spectator had been caught in the eye and, in between spasms on the floor, was wailing and clutching at the gooey mess that had once been home to her eye. It was not long before another shard caught the blonde woman deep in her remaining eye, leaving a gruesome pool of thick mess slipping between her fingers. It was the last image Robert had of Polly, the once bubbly, eager to learn student.

A deafening crack filled the entire room, the shaking intensified, and the dust showered down decorating hair, smothering and choking airways. Then, from the back wall, an angel wing gave way, crashing down atop two men attempting to make their way to one of the stone thrones. A bone crunching thud followed by a murky white cloud of dust hit everyone like a train. The plume of dust first engulfed Anastasia and Doctor Lazeele, still completely unaware of what was going on around them, focussed only on each other. Then, finally, it hit everyone else, devouring the entire stone table, eating away at the room, picking the occupants off one by one. Robert raised an arm to his face, shielding his eyes as the mud, dust, and shards of stone flew into him, cutting him like a thousand tiny blades, that seemed to last an eternity. Screams echoed in his ears above the blustering wind and the electric zaps, screams of agony and pain, which then made way for crackling and bubbling. Finally, when the smell of stone and concrete dust had subsided, the stench of burned toast, singed hair, and roasted pork filled the air. An enormous heat hit Robert as the room filled with grey and orange dust, with sparks of brilliant dazzling yellow flew from the dense cloud in front of him. Then there was silence.

Chapter 6 – From the Ashes

After a couple of minutes, Robert lowered his arm, allowing his eyes to adjust to the dimly lit room. Small explosions and cute, gorgeous bright yellow sparks danced from the edges of the room from broken flickering lights embedded in the ceiling, broken electricity cables fell from the ceiling with small yellow fires raging away at the ends of each one, with a low erratic buzz filling the empty quietness. There was just enough light to allow Robert to see the horrors before him.

Scorched cadavers, still smoking, littered the floor, burned, blackened arms reaching to the heavens. The putrid smell and the sight made Robert feel sick and he wretched over what once resembled a stone chair, now it formed a pile of dust. Large chunks of stones had flattened some of the corpses, vile brown stains seeped from under the jagged rocks. The blackened figures that were still visible were completely indistinguishable, their faces charred, their clothes burned away leaving twisted, puss-ridden corpses reaching for the heavens. No discernible features could be picked out. Vibrant red pockets poked out from underneath cracked skin, with ugly white, yellow, and green gloopy fluid, and thick red pools leaking out. Yet, Robert knew who were next to him. His entire team, now reduced to rotting, broken statues, on their knees, on their sides, on their stomachs, with half an arm, or one leg, forever crying out for the rest of time in this torturous tomb.

The once pristine, smooth stone room was now broken and desecrated. Cracks climbed high on the stone walls, the symbol at the back was malformed, missing nearly half the wing and cross. Parts of the room had fallen in on itself, leaving piles of grey rubble all around. Robert wiped his face; dust and bits of stone and gravel fell away. His hand came away painted completely covered in an ashen white powder.

A ray of sunlight entered through a small pocket towards the end of the room where the ceiling had completely given way, the first time this tomb had ever seen natural light. Robert counted the corpses, seventeen in total that he could see, including the bodies that had been crushed in half. There were two bodies that he had seen crushed by one of the beautiful wings that had been eaten by the floor. Towards the back of the room, a gloriously designed golden wing was being swallowed by the floor. When it had fallen from its holding, a huge crater had been formed in the floor. Now the tip of the wing reached only the height of the table which had also been sawn in half by falling debris, making it look like a sinking ship. Robert inspected the end of the table briefly, his thick rubber boots thudding along the dusty floor, leaving large imprints as he went. What stunned Robert was this area was strangely absent of death. Doctor Lazeele and Doctor Maxwell-Heart's bodies were nowhere to be seen. They had vanished, unless they had been crushed, which did not appear to be the case as no stones had come near this end of the table. Even the small corpse of Doctor Langley appeared to have gone missing.

Robert coughed and wheezed violently as he breathed in the dust-ridden air. The stench of rot and roasted flesh was getting worse, he pulled a sleeve up to his mouth and held in vomit. He turned and made his way to the elevator exit: he could not stand the sight or the stench any longer. Where he was going to go, or how he was going to leave he did not know, all he knew was he had to get out. What had just happened remained a mystery to him. Why was he spared? He supposed this was the end of *Densissimus Imminebat* with the death of their remaining members and the ominous disappearance of the last of their big wigs. Was that really a bad thing though, Robert mused? His head was brimming with questions he was sure he would die with, maybe if he could find that guide that brought him to this coffin, he would be able to make his way out, but what would he tell her? Would she not ask where everyone else was? Was she responsible for this? He could only find out he supposed. He just hoped that was the last he had ever heard of that damned Lazeele Mineral.

Robert stumbled back to where this horror had all begun for him, to the doors of the elevator. His mouth was dry and rough. Dust congealed inside his mouth and all over his tongue, making the inside of his mouth feel like sandpaper. Every breathe he took got harder and harder as he inhaled a sea of concrete. He now wished for the water that had smashed and gone everywhere in the chaos.

Finally, he reached salvation! Robert reached the wall that he had entered through what felt like so long ago. Awkwardly upon the wall was a small matte silver pad with a dim flashing red button on it. Pressing the button with a bulging snow white thumb he allowed himself a little sigh of relief to escape his lips. *It will soon all be* over.

Removing his thick thumb, the button fizzed as glistening orange sparks flew out all around him with small pops and crackles, teasing him as a small plume of white-grey smoke rose to the small hatch in the ceiling above, reaching for the heavens. Robert recoiled, shaking his hand, pulling it close to his chest, it was on fire as static ran through his forearm. The top of his thumb had turned black. Robert watched in utter dismay and confusion as the silver pad was consumed by small orange flames that licked at the wall around it. Turning his back on the elevator, his eyes settled on a sliver of warm sunlight beaming through a small crack in the ceiling. Confusion turned to rage, then rage gave way to hopelessness. He turned back to the elevator door and fell to his knees, resting his head against the door. He let out a whimper and a sob, tears began to fall down his cheeks stinging, burning his skin, as he desperately tried to think of a way out. Slowly he ran out of tears, and he soon ran out of ideas. Then it was time for another round of sobbing.

Dreams of insanity came to Robert through the tears. His mind was piecing a puzzle together that did not exist. In front of the stricken man came a citadel, rife with life, basking in a gorgeous orange glow. Building stretched for miles and towers touched the sky. Soon the glow turned to unforgiving flames, the citadel lit up in hellish fire until all that was left was a forest green smog layering the great city. A darkness that nothing could escape descended, where demons, ghouls and the dead came to play. Then, to Roberts incredulous mind's eye stood a magnificent pyramid. Before it knelt a hundred to a thousand onlookers in front of grey tombs and headstones. Within the pyramid, a child, puppeteering all those who worshipped her. A small, simple golden crown sat atop her head of straw-like hair; a third eye sat in the middle of her small forehead. Next to her, laid a woman with fiery red hair, her black-nailed hands laid on her chest, crossed, her eyes shut tight. Slowly, the girl raised her arms. In response, the beautiful red-haired woman slowly rose from her slumber, and before the pyramid crawling from their graves and breaking out of their tombs came... Robert slapped himself. Already he was falling into insane hallucinations.

Gradually the sunlight faded away. The darkness came to claim its next victim. Robert slowly withered away leaning against the wall hunched over in the foetal position, giving up hope. His only solace, the sunlight, was quickly fading, the terrors of the night were beginning to consume him. As the looming night arrived, so too did the distant giggling of a child, so silent at first, but it was there. As the night wore on, and Robert's mind started to melt in a litany of agony, desperation and hopelessness, the giggling built into a crescendo, taunting Robert. The giggling child was now Robert's only companion on a never-ending pathway to nowhere.

To Be Continued

Author's Notes

This is a massive achievement for me. I cannot begin to tell you how happy I am to be at this stage with my first story. It has taken a long time to get to this point. Perhaps setting unrealistic goals contributed to this and my everyday life also playing a part. However, to finally say I have published a book fills me with an immense sense of pride.

Starting off, I began work on this huge idea. Gradually, I have come to break this apart and begin splitting some of the ideas into short stories, branching them off to become their own body of work. Of course, I still have a huge novel in the works, but this will take some time.

I had incredible fun writing this and I hope you all had fun reading it. I am still enjoying myself and have begun work on two more books and indeed one is near completion. Hopefully this means there is not too long to wait for the next release.

I have many people to thank and simply this small section would not be big enough to fit everyone in. So, I will simply say thank you to everyone who has supported me, from my close family to my partner, and friends. To be honest, I feel like that does not do anyone justice, but if anyone takes offence then I shall amend it when my next work is released, I promise!

Finally, a short note on what to expect from my upcoming stories. The Artist of Offerton Manor is nearing completion and is in the editing process. This is a standalone work and is a completely different genre that I wanted to experiment with. I have tried to incorporate horror elements to it, while also sprinkling in a bit of a crime thriller style to it. Let's see how this pans out.
Within this series though (Tales of the Ascension), there are still many more works to come. I have started on two more stories, with Citadel of the Dead the closest, but still some way to go. Many will be around this length; however some will be bigger. Darktrace Hotel, the big novel I am very far along with, is already well over the wordcount of this story.

Now, this is my last note, I promise. If you have got this far, well done! But also, I hope you have enjoyed this story and I hope you are as excited as I am to continue this journey and find out where this takes us. There are some huge things to come and I cannot wait to share them with you all.

Thank you,

Ben Aldous
February 2024

Coming soon

Tales of the Ascension Series:

Citadel of the Dead

The Fires of Arol

Separate Story

The Artist of Offerton Manor

Printed in Great Britain
by Amazon